Gorgeous!

First published in 1999

1 3 5 7 9 10 8 6 4 2

© Text Caroline Castle 1999
© Illustrations Sam Childs 1999

Caroline Castle and Sam Childs have asserted their right under
the Copyright, Designs and Patents Act, 1988, to be identified
as the author and illustrator of this work

First published in the United Kingdom in 1999 by
Hutchinson Children's Books
Random House UK Limited
20 Vauxhall Bridge Road, London SW1V 2SA

Random House Australia (Pty) Limited
20 Alfred Street, Milsons Point, Sydney
New South Wales 2061, Australia

Random House New Zealand Limited
18 Poland Road, Glenfield
Auckland 10, New Zealand

Random House South Africa (Pty) Limited
Endulini, 5A Jubilee Road, Parktown 2193, South Africa

Random House UK Limited Reg. No. 954009

A CIP catalogue record for this book is available from
the British Library

ISBN: 0 09 176874 8

Printed in Hong Kong by Midas Printing Limited

Gorgeous!

Caroline Castle & Sam Childs

HUTCHINSON

London Sydney Auckland Johannesburg

One morning Big Zeb had a feeling
something wonderful was going to happen.

So she disappeared behind a bush
to be by herself.

'Ouch!'

'Hello, Little Zeb.'

Little Zeb was brand spanking new.

He twitched his nose.

He blinked his eyes.

He swished his tail and he made a small squeaky noise.

'Gorgeous!' said Big Zeb.
'Tip top.' And she gave him
a big lick behind his ears.

Then Little Zeb trotted off after Big Zeb
on his brand new legs that went
clippity-clop, clippity-clop.
'Gorgeous,' he said, 'tip top,'
because he liked the sound
and because they were the
only words he knew.

Big Zeb and Little Zeb joined the herd.
'Gorgeous!' cried the other zebras when
they saw Big Zeb's pride and joy. 'Tip top!'
Then the big herd of zebras set off on their
journey across the plains.
'Now stick with me baby,' said Big Zeb,
'and you'll be all right.'

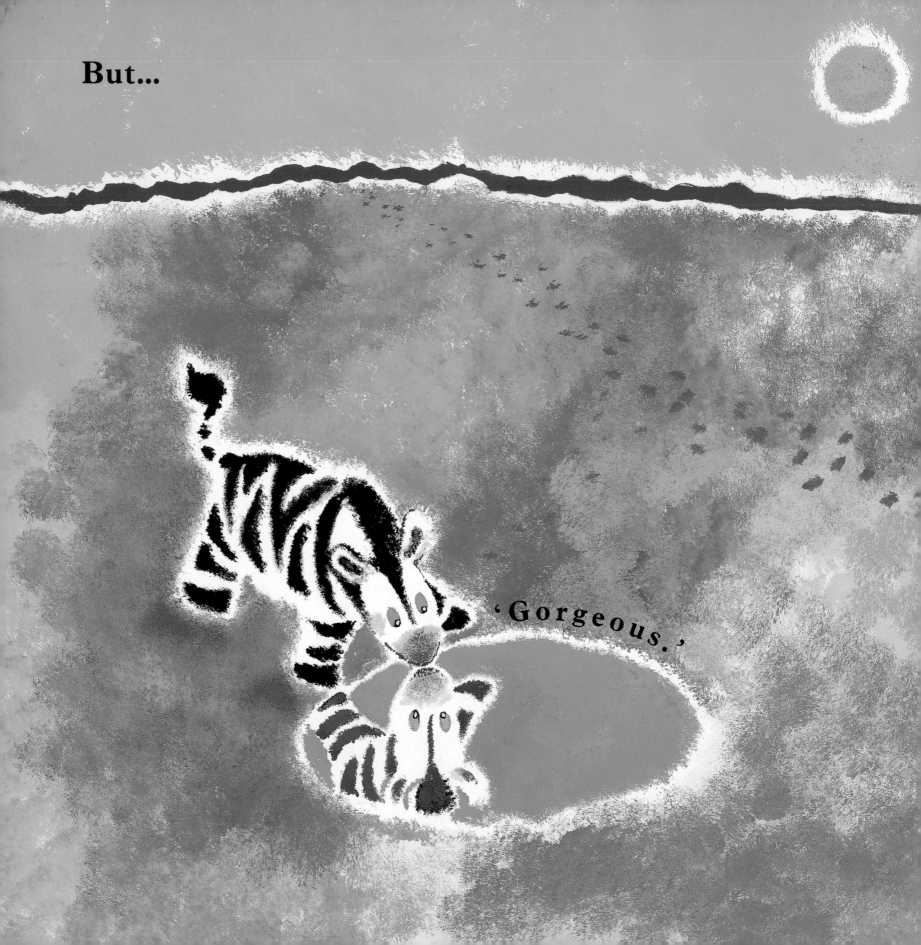

But...

'Gorgeous.'

'Grrrrr

Suddenly there was a roaring and a grumbling and a rumbling and a growling.

And Little Zeb was all alone.

'r!' went the lion.

'Gorgeous!' said Little Zeb happily.

'*What?*' said the lion.

'Gorgeous!' said Little Zeb again. 'Stick with me baby and you'll be all right.'

And he gave the lion a big slobbery lick behind his ears. 'Tip top.'

'Oh really?' said the lion. And he flicked his tail and bristled his mane and did a proud little dance.

But then he
remembered
he was a lion.

'Grrrrrr!'

And a hungry lion at that!

Big Zeb was there in a flash.
'Get lost!' she cried.

'Get lost gorgeous!' shouted Little Zeb.

'**Vamoosh!**' shouted Big Zeb and she kicked that lion's bottom and sent him on his way.

'Poooosh, tip top!' cried Little Zeb
with his brand new voice.

Little Zeb trotted off behind Big Zeb on his brand
new clippy-cloppy, springy-zingy legs.

Back with the herd Big Zeb
looked at Little Zeb sternly.
'*Not* gorgeous!' she said,
nodding her head at the
lion's bottom as it
disappeared into the trees.
'*Danger,*' growled Big Zeb
in a big gruff voice.
'*Danger,*' said Little Zeb gravely
in a new growly voice. '*Not* gorgeous.'

That night under the great
starry sky Little Zeb tried
out all his new words.

'Gorgeous.'

'*Not* gorgeous.'

'Stick with
me baby and
you'll be all right.'

'Danger.'

'Vamooooosh!'

Big Zeb trotted up
and wrapped her great big
warmth all around Little Zeb.
'Mmmmmmm,' she said.
'Mmmmmmmmmmm,'
sang Little Zeb happily.
'Tip top gorgeous!'